To all the real-life unicorns
who believe that we are all unique,
divine, and magical

The Most Magical Time of the Year!

April Showers
Illustrated by Anthony Conley

Random House New York

 Published in the United States by Random House Children's Books,
a division of Penguin Random House LLC, New York.

Library of Congress Cataloging-in-Publication Data is available upon request.
ISBN 978-0-593-70412-7 (hardcover) — ISBN 978-0-593-70413-4 (lib. bdg.) — ISBN 978-0-593-70414-1 (ebook)
MANUFACTURED IN CHINA
10 9 8 7 6 5 4 3 2
First Edition

Winter had arrived in the enchanted land of Afronia! Unique, Divine, and Magical couldn't wait to fill their Holiday Magic Kindness Countdown calendars: one sticker for each day they performed an act of kindness.

Unique sang happily:

"The first day of December is finally here!
Time to spread joy and holiday cheer!"

Everyone was eager for Santa to arrive and pick up their holiday letters.

The castle sparkled with lights, while tiny bells jingled from pine boughs in the courtyard. And tall stacks of uniyum pies were ready to eat!

Magical had asked Unique and Divine to use their superpowers to welcome Santa.

Unique was working on a super-song, and Divine would use her super-strength to present the big sack of letters. Magical, who could see the goodness in everyone's heart, had known they were the perfect choice to help!

"Santa's coming *today*!" Magical said. She couldn't wait to see her old friend.

"But my kindness song's not done! Please—I need more time!" Unique said.

"You always sing what's in your heart," Magical reassured her. "And your heart *sparkles* with the kindness of Christmas."

"You can do it, Unique!" added Divine.

Unique tried out her new song:

"Sing with me, friends; hear my call:
welcome Santa, one and all.
Magical and divine, that's what we all are.
We help spread kindness, near and far!"

Soon, everyone was singing. As they sang louder, all of Afronia began to glow with Christmas spirit.

Suddenly they heard an enchanted "Ho, ho, ho!" as Santa's sleigh flew in.

Divine's and Unique's horns sparkled with excitement. This really was the most magical time of the year!

“Greetings, friends of Afronia,” Santa said. “Thank you for the beautiful song! You are so kind to welcome me.”

Divine used her super-strength to present Santa with the giant sack of letters.

As Santa loaded the letters onto his sleigh, he asked Magical to lead Afronia's Holiday Magic Kindness Countdown.

"I would be honored!" Magical said.

Santa gave them each a big, shiny present. "Open this on Christmas Eve, when your kindness calendars are full. . . ."

Unique, Divine, and Magical couldn't wait to open the sparkly packages. But more importantly, they knew that spreading kindness was the perfect way to spend the days until Christmas.

For the rest of the month, the unicorns found many ways to be kind. They cooked food for their friends. They decorated neighbors' houses. They helped out wherever they could. And Unique even wrote a special song!

"Share the kindness of Christmas right from the start. The best gifts come straight from the heart."

Finally, on Christmas Eve, they opened the big presents from Santa.

They were filled with magical ornaments!

“Working together and showing kindness have made the season much more special,” said Divine.

This Christmas truly was *magical.*

MERRY CHRISTMAS and HAPPY HOLIDAYS!
Be kind in every way!

DECEMBER

Holiday Magic Kindness Countdown Calendar

The holidays are the perfect time to spread kindness, love, and joy!
Whenever you complete an act of kindness, add a sticker to that day.

1	2	3	4	5	6	7
8	9	10	11	12	13	14
15	16	17	18	19	20	21
22	23	24	25	26	27	28
29	30	31